MAMA'S NIGHTINGALE

A Story of Immigration and Separation

by Edwidge Danticat · *illustrations by* Leslie Staub

DIAL BOOKS FOR YOUNG READERS
an imprint of Penguin Group (USA) LLC

DIAL BOOKS FOR YOUNG READERS
Published by the Penguin Group
Penguin Group (USA) LLC
375 Hudson Street
New York, New York 10014

USA * Canada * UK * Ireland * Australia
New Zealand * India * South Africa * China
penguin.com
A Penguin Random House Company

Library of Congress Cataloging-in-Publication Data

Danticat, Edwidge, date.
Mama's nightingale : a story of immigration and separation / by Edwidge Danticat ; illustrated by Leslie Staub.   pages cm
Summary: When Saya's mother is sent to jail as an illegal immigrant, she sends her daughter a cassette tape with a song
and a bedtime story, which inspires Saya to write a story of her own—one that just might bring her mother home.
ISBN 978-0-525-42809-1 (hardcover)
[1. Mothers and daughters—Fiction. 2. Separation (Psychology)—Fiction. 3. Detention of persons—Fiction.
4. Emigration and immigration—Fiction. 5. Haitian Americans—Fiction.] I. Staub, Leslie, date, – illustrator. II. Title.

PZ7.D2385Mam 2015   [E]—dc23   2014039868

Manufactured in China on acid-free paper

1 3 5 7 9 10 8 6 4 2

Designed by Mina Chung · Text set in Cooper Oldstyle
This art was created using oil paint.

For Nara and Liz,
   with love and gratitude
                —ED

To Renee and Kris with big, big love
                —LS

Tanpri kite bon ti nouvèl pou nou!

When Mama first goes away,
what I miss most is the sound of
her voice.

At night, while Papa's asleep, I
sneak out of bed to listen to Mama's
greeting on our answering machine.

"*Tanpri kite bon ti nouvèl pou
nou!*" Please, leave us good news!

Tanpri kite bon ti nouvèl pou nou!

One night, I accidentally erase the greeting, and I can no longer hear Mama say those cheerful words that always make me feel so warm inside.

We have no good news.

For the last three months, Mama's been at Sunshine Correctional, a prison for women without papers.

When I ask Papa, "What kind of papers does Mama need?" he says, "Papers that say she belongs in this country."

"Can Mama have *my* papers?" I ask.

She can't.

When I ask Papa, "When is Mama coming home?" he says, "You know, Saya, Mama loves you *anpil, anpil,* very, very much. She'd never stay away too long, if she could help it."

Every night after he makes dinner for us and helps me with my homework, Papa sits at the kitchen table and writes letters to the judges who send people without papers to jail. He also writes to our mayor and congresswoman and all the newspapers and television reporters he's ever heard of. No one ever writes him back.

Papa and I visit Mama every week.

When she sees me, Mama runs to me, picks me up, and hugs me real tight.

"I miss you, Wosiyòl," Mama says, while pretending to bite my cheeks.

Wosiyòl is Mama's nickname for me.

In Mama's Haitian stories, a *wosiyòl* is a beautiful nightingale who loves the taste of a sweet cottony fruit called a soursop. Just like I do. The *wosiyòl* also keeps mean old witches from eating little children by distracting them with her beautiful song.

Mama leans over and hums the *wosiyòl*'s song in my ear. The melody is as soft as Mama's touch and as sweet as a real soursop.

When Mama stops humming, she asks me about school and whether Papa and I are taking good care of each other. I sit on her lap and breathe in the smell of coconut pomade in her hair as she and Papa talk.

"Gotta go, folks," one of the guards says when it's time to take
Mama away.

I kick and I scream and beg to stay with her.

Tears run down Mama's face as she is led away.

The two guards on either side of her give me very stern looks. One of them
tells Papa not to bring me again until I can behave myself.

In the car on the way home, I miss Mama so much
my belly aches. I fall asleep and dream of the visit,
except in my dream, Mama comes home with Papa and me.

A few days later, a package arrives in the mail from Mama.
In the envelope is a letter for Papa, and for me a cassette with a card that says,
"Yon istwa dodo pou Saya," a bedtime story for Saya.

That night, Papa tucks me in, then puts his old tape recorder by my bed.
It's exactly like the one he brought to Mama when she was first taken to jail.
He pushes the PLAY button and tiptoes out of my room.

Suddenly the room is filled with Mama's wind-chime voice singing about the soursop and the nightingale. At the end of the song, Mama tells me a new bedtime story, one she made up herself. It's about a mommy nightingale who goes on a very long journey and is looking for a rainbow trail in the sky so she can return home to her baby nightingale.

I close my eyes and imagine Mama lying next to me as she leans in to whisper the nightingale's story in my ear. I imagine Mama tucking me in, kissing me good night, then going to sleep in the next room with Papa.

The next time we visit Mama, I do my best not to cry. I sit on her lap and kiss her whole face. I don't ask when she's coming home, because she doesn't know either.

After that visit, a new tape with a new story arrives at the house every week. Sometimes the stories are as sad as melted ice cream. Other times they are as happy as a whole day at the beach.

One day, I sit next to Papa while he is writing one of his many long letters. We listen to Mama's voice together.

When the room is quiet again, I ask Papa, "When is Mama coming home?"

He looks like he is going to get angry, but then he bites his lower lip.

"You know, Saya, Mama loves you *anpil*, *anpil*, very, very much," he begins telling me, then stops.

He suddenly looks sadder than sad, as though Mama might never come home again.

"Papa, can I write letters, too?" I ask.

"Of course," he says. "You can write your own story."

I take Papa's advice, sit down, and write my own story.

When I am done, Papa sends what I have written to one of the newspaper reporters he's been writing to.

A few days later, there is a message on our answering machine. The message is from a lady reporter saying that she wants to print my story in the newspaper for everyone to read!

The next day, another reporter comes to our apartment to interview Papa and me for the television news.

With a big lump in my throat, I tell her how much I miss Mama and how I wish she could be with us again.

Papa tells the television reporter how Mama was arrested by the immigration police while working in a restaurant. And how she might be sent back to Haiti at any time. Mama came to America before she met Papa, and before I was born, and she doesn't have the right papers.

Not yet anyway.

NEWS 2

In a week's time, because of
all the phone calls and the letters
to the prison from people who read about
us in the newspaper and saw us on TV, Mama is
brought before a judge.

The judge says Mama can come home
with Papa and me while she is waiting for
her papers.

Sitting in the courtroom with Papa,
I'm so happy and proud I feel like running up
to the bench and giving the judge a big hug.

Finally Mama is home with us again.

At bedtime, Mama asks me which of her stories I would most like to hear. I pick my favorite one: the one about the mommy nightingale who skips over rainbows, trying to get home.

"How does the story end?" I ask Mama, even though I already know the answer.

"A smart and brave little nightingale helps her mommy find the right rainbow trail," Mama says. "And the mommy follows it home."

I like the way Mama's and my story ends, too.

I like that it is our words that brought us together again.

Author's Note

I grew up in a family that was separated, in part, by immigration. For most of my childhood, my parents were living in the United States while my brother Bob and I were living with my aunt and uncle in Haiti. I knew that my parents wanted to send for us, but we were always told that they couldn't because they didn't have the right papers. This idea of having the right papers has always fascinated me.

As children in Haiti, my brother and I sometimes played writing games, making up passports, visas, and other documents that might one day reunite us with our parents.

Living in Miami now, with two young daughters of my own, I meet a lot of children who are separated from either one or both of their parents because their parents are undocumented, or as Saya says, are "without papers." According to the United States' Department of Homeland Security's Immigrations and Customs Enforcement (ICE), the people Saya refers to as the immigration police, over 70,000 parents of American-born children have been jailed and deported in recent years.

This book is dedicated to those children, who, like Saya, are dreaming of the day when their mother, or father, or both parents, will come home.